The dragon's boy

Yolen, Jane

Points: 4.0

Test#: 0000

Lvl: 5.9

THE
DRAGON'S BOY

THE DRAGON'S BOY

by Jane Yolen

■ HarperCollins*Publishers*

Typography by Joyce Hopkins

Library of Congress Cataloging-in-Publication Data
Yolen, Jane.
    The dragon's boy / by Jane Yolen.
        p.   cm.
    Summary: Young Arthur meets a dragon and comes to accept him as a friend and mentor.
    ISBN 0-06-026789-5.—ISBN·0-06-026790-9 (lib. bdg.)
    [1. Arthur, King—Fiction.   2. Merlin (Legendary character)—Fiction.]   I. Title.
PZ7.Y78Ds   1990   89-24642
[Fic]—dc20   CIP
                                                            AC

For David, in memory of our months in Scotland,
and Heidi, Adam, and Jason, who stayed at home,
getting wisdom.

Contents

THE
DRAGON'S BOY

1

The Cave in the Fens

It was on a day in early spring, with the clouds scudding across a gray sky, promising a rain that never quite fell, that Artos found the cave.

"Hullo," he whispered to himself, a habit he'd gotten into as he so often had no one else to talk to.

He hadn't been looking for a cave but rather chasing after Sir Ector's brachet hound Boadie, the one who always slipped her chain to go after hare. She'd slipped Artos as well, speeding down the cobbled path and out the castle's small back gate, the Cowgate. Luckily he'd caught sight of her as she whipped around the corner of it, and on and off he'd seen her coursing until they'd come to the boggy wasteland north of the castle. Then he'd lost her for good and could only follow by her tracks.

If she hadn't been Sir Ector's prize brachet and ready to whelp for the first time, he'd have left her there and trudged back to the castle in disgust, knowing she'd eventually find her way home, with or without any hare. But he feared she might lose her pups out there in the bogs, and then he'd get whipped double, once for letting her get away and once for the loss of the litter. So he spent the better part of the morning following her tracks, crossing and recrossing a small, cold, meandering stream and occasionally wading thigh deep in the water.

He let out his own stream of curses, much milder than any the rough men in the castle used. But they were heartfelt curses against both the chill of the water and the fact that, if he'd been one of the other boys—Bedvere or Lancot or Sir Ector's true son, Cai—the water would have only been up to his knees. They'd all gotten their growth earlier than he. Indeed, despite Sir Ector's gruff promises that he would be tallest of them all, Artos despaired of ever getting any bigger. At thirteen surely he deserved to be higher than Lady Marion's shoulder.

"Knees or thighs," he reminded himself, unconsciously mimicking Sir Ector's mumbling accent, "it's blessed cold." He climbed out of the stream and up the slippery bank.

Despite the cold, his fair hair lay matted with sweat against the back of his head, the wet strands looking nearly black. There was a streak of mud against the right side of his nose, deposited there when he'd rubbed his eye with a grimy fist. His cheeks, naturally pale, were flushed from the run.

The sun was exactly overhead, its corona lighting the edges of the clouds. Noon—and he hadn't eaten since breakfast, a simple bowl of milk swallowed hastily before the sun was even up. His stomach growled at the thought. Rubbing a fist against his belly to quiet it, he listened for the hound's baying.

It was dead still.

"I knew it!" he whispered angrily. "She's gone home." He could easily imagine her in the kennelyard, slopping up food, her feet and belly dry. The thought of being dry and fed made his own stomach yowl again. This time he pounded against it three times. The growling stopped.

Nevertheless, the brachet was his responsibility. He had to search for her till he was sure. Putting his fingers to his mouth, he let out a shrill whistle that ordinarily would have brought Boadie running.

There was no answer, and except for the sound of the wind puzzling across the fenland, there was a complete silence.

The fen was a low, hummocky place full of brown pools and quaking mosses; and in the slow, floating waters there was an abundance of duckweed and frog-bit, mile after mile of it looking the same. From where he stood, low down amongst the lumpy mosses, he couldn't see the castle, not even a glimpse of one of the two towers. And with the sun straight overhead, he wasn't sure which way was north or which way south.

Not that he thought he was lost.

"Never lost—just bothered a bit!" he said aloud, using the favorite phrase of the Master of Hounds, a whey-colored man with a fringe of white hair. The sound of the phrase comforted him. If he wasn't lost—only bothered—he'd be home soon, his wet boots off and drying in front of a warm peatfire.

Turning slowly, Artos stared across the fens. His boots were sinking slowly in the shaking, muddy land. It took an effort to raise them, one after another. Each time he did, they made an awful sucking noise, like the Master of Hounds at his soup, only louder. At the last turn, he saw behind him a small tor mounding up over the bog, dog tracks running up it.

"If I climb that," he encouraged himself, "I'll be able to see what I need to see." He meant, of course, he'd be able to see the castle from the small hillock and judge the distance home, maybe even locate a drier route. His feet were really cold now, the water having gotten in over the tops of his boots in the stream and squishing up between his toes at every step. Not that the boots mattered. They were an old pair, Cai's castoffs, and had never really fit anyway. But he still didn't fancy walking all the way back squishing like that.

He'd never been on his own this far north of the castle before and certainly never would have planned coming out into the watery fens where the peat hags reigned. They could pull a big shire horse down, not even bothering to spit back the bones. Everyone knew that.

"Blasted dog!" he swore again, hotly. "Blasted Boadie!" He felt a little better having said it aloud.

If the little tor had been a mountain he wouldn't have attempted it. Certainly neither he nor any of the other boys would dare go up the High Tor, which was the large mount northwest of the castle. It was craggy, with sheer sides, its top usually hidden in the mists. There was no easy path up. The High Tor had an evil reputation, Cai said. Princes who tried to climb it were still there, locked in the stone. Lancot said he'd heard how the High King's only son had been whisked away there the day he'd been born and devoured by witches for their All Hallow's meal. Bedvere had only recently recalled a rhyme his old Nanny Bess had taught him: "Up the Tor, Life's nae more."

But of course the hillock wasn't *that* tor and it *would* be the perfect place from which to get his bearings. So he slogged toward it, threading through the hummocks and the tussocky grass, forcing himself not to mind the water squishing up between his toes, following the tracks.

He was halfway up the tor and halfway around it as well when he saw the cave.

"Hullo!" he whispered.

It was only an unprepossessing black hole in the rock and only a bit higher than himself, as round and as smooth as if it had been carved out by a master hand. The opening was shaped into a rock that was as gray and slatey as the sky. There wasn't a single grain or vein running across the rockface to distinguish it, and Boadie's tracks had disappeared.

Nervously he ran his fingers through the tangles of his hair, his gooseberry-colored eyes wide. Then he stepped through the dark doorway. He went less out of courage than curiosity, being particularly careful of some long, spearlike rocks hanging from the ceiling of the cave just two steps beyond the opening.

Slowly his eyes got used to the dark and he began to make out a grayer, mistier color from the black. Suddenly forgetting dog and castle and the mud in his boots, he thought he might have a go at exploring. The Master of Hounds had always warned him that he'd a "big bump of curiosity," as if that were a particularly bad thing to own. *But*, he reasoned, *if you're the youngest and the slightest, what else do you have of any use except imagination and curiosity?* And so thinking, he stepped even farther into the cave.

That was when, standing ever so quiet and trying to make out the outlines of the place, he heard the breathing. At first he thought it was his own. But when he took a deep gulp of air and held it, the sound still went on. It wasn't very loud, except that the cave had a strange magnifying power, and so he was able to hear every rumbling bit of it. It was low and steady, almost like a cat's purr, except there was an occasional *pop!* serving as punctuation. It was—he was quite sure—a snore. And he knew from that snore that whatever made it had to be very large. He also knew that the Master of Hounds had been quite right in warning him about his curiosity. Suddenly he had quite enough of exploring.

He began to back out of the cave slowly, quietly, when he came bang up against something that smacked his head hard. And though he managed not to cry out, the stone rang in what seemed to be twenty different tones and, abruptly, the snore stopped.

"Blast!" Artos swore under his breath. He put a hand to the back of his head, which hurt horribly, and one in front of him to ward off whatever it was that was attached to that loud, breathy snore; for whatever it was was surely awake now.

"STAAAAAAAY!" came a low, rumbling command.

He stopped at once and, for a stuttering moment, so did his heart.

2

The Master of Wisdoms

Before Artos could move, that awful voice began again.

"Whoooooooooo are you?" It was less an echo this time and more an elongated sigh.

Biting his lip, Artos answered in a voice that broke several times in odd places. "I am nobody, really, just Artos. A fosterling. From Sir Ector's castle." He turned slightly and gestured toward the cave entrance, outside, where presumably the castle still stood. He turned back and added, hastily, "Sir."

A low rumbling, more like another snore than

a sentence, was all that answered him. It was such a surprisingly homey sound that it freed him of his terror long enough to ask, "And who are you?" He hesitated. "Sir?"

Something creaked. There was an odd clanking. Then the voice, augmented almost tenfold, boomed at him: "I AM THE GREAT RIDDLER. I AM THE MASTER OF WISDOMS. I AM THE WORD AND I AM THE LIGHT. I WAS AND AM AND WILL BE."

Artos nearly fainted from the noise. He put his right hand before him as if to hold back the overpowering sound and bit his lip again. This time he drew blood. Wondering if blood would arouse the beast further, he sucked it away quickly. Then, when the echoes of that ghastly voice ended, Artos whispered, "Are you a hermit, sir? An anchorite? Are you a Druid priest? A penitent knight?" He knew such beings sometimes inhabited caves, but even he knew the guesses were stupid for that great noise was surely no mere man's voice. However, he hoped that by asking he might encourage whatever it was to some kind of gentleness. Or pity.

The great whisper that answered him came in a rush of wind: *"I Am The Dragon!"*

"Oh!" Artos said.

"Is that all you can say?" the dragon asked peevishly. "I tell you I Am The Dragon and all you can answer is *oh?*"

Artos was silent.

The great breathy voice sighed. "Sit down, boy. It's been a long time since I've had company in my cave. A long time and a lonely time."

Artos was sure that the one thing he'd better *not* do was sit. Sitting would make him vulnerable, an easy prey. Sitting could be prelude to . . . to . . . but here his vaunted imagination failed him. All he could do was stutter. "But . . . but . . . but . . ." It was not a good beginning.

"No *buts*," said the dragon.

"But," Artos began again, desperately needing to uphold his end of the conversation. *A talking dragon,* he told himself, *is not an eating dragon. Perhaps if I explain that I am sure to be missed back at the castle, now, this very moment . . .*

"Shush boy, and listen. I will pay for your visit."

Artos sat, plunking himself down on a small riser of stone. It wasn't greed that kept him there. Rather, it was the thought that if he was to be paid, then hunger *wasn't* the dragon's object and therefore he, Artos, was *not* to be dinner.

"So, young Artos of Sir Ector's castle, how

14

would you like to be paid—in gold, in jewels, or in wisdom?"

A sudden flame from the center of the cave lit up the interior and, for the first time, Artos could see that there were jewels scattered about the floor amongst the rocks and pebbles. Jewels! But then, as suddenly as the flame, came the terrible thought: *Dragons are known to be the finest games players in the world. It has named itself The Great Riddler. Perhaps if I don't answer correctly, I'll be eaten after all.*

Artos could feel sweat running down the back of his neck. His feet, so long forgotten, felt squishy and cold inside the wet boots. He had a strange ache at the base of his skull, a throbbing at his temple. But then cunning, an old habit, claimed him. Like most small people, he had a genius for escape. Rarely had the bigger boys played more than one trick on him, though he'd never gotten his own back against them.

"Wisdom, sir," he said. It was the least likely to appeal to a greedy sort, and therefore most likely to be the right answer, though he'd really rather have had gold or jewels. "Wisdom."

Another bright flame spouted from the cave center. "An excellent choice," the dragon said.

Artos let himself relax but only a little, for he hardly expected the game would be won this easily.

"Excellent," the dragon repeated. "And I've been needing a boy just your age for some time."

Not to eat! Artos thought wildly. *Perhaps I'd better point out how small I am, how thin.*

But the dragon went on as if it had no idea of the terror it had just instilled in Artos. "A boy to pass my wisdom on to. So listen well, young Artos of Sir Ector's castle."

Artos didn't move and hoped the dragon wouldn't notice how everything—*everything*—about him had suddenly, inexplicably, relaxed. Perhaps the dragon would take the silence to mean that Artos was listening when Artos knew it really meant that he couldn't have moved now even if he wanted to. His hands were limp, his feet were limp, even his nose felt limp. He could scarcely breathe through it. All he *could* do was listen.

"My word of wisdom for the day," the dragon began, "is this: *Old dragons like old thorns can still prick.* And I am a very old dragon. So take care."

Limply, Artos whispered back, "Yes, sir." But

16

a part of him worried over that wisdom, picking away at it as if it were a bit of torn skin next to a fingernail. It was familiar, that wisdom. *Why was it so familiar?* And then he had it: The dragon's wisdom was very similar to a bit of wit he'd heard often enough on the village streets, only there it went slightly differently. It was old priests, not old dragons, the villagers warned about. He couldn't for the life of him think why the two should be the same. *For the life of him.* That, he knew, was a bad phrase at a time like this. Aloud, all he said was, "I shall remember, sir."

"Good. I'm sure you will," the dragon said. "And now, as a reward . . ."

"A reward?" He spoke without thinking.

"A reward for being such a good listener. You may take that small jewel—there."

The strange clanking accompanied the extension of a gigantic scaled foot. The foot had four toes each the size of Artos' thighs; there were three toes in the front, one in the back. The foot scrabbled along the cave floor, clacketing and rattling, then stopped close to Artos.

Too close, he thought, but he was too terrified

to stand up and run, though inside he drew himself as far away from the foot as was possible, a kind of mental shrinking.

The nail from the center toe began to extend outward. It was a curved, steel-colored blade, reflecting in the light of the dragon's fiery breath. It stopped with an odd click, then tapped a red jewel the size of a leek bulb.

"There!" the dragon said again. "Go on, boy. Take it."

Wondering if this were yet another test, Artos hesitated and the dragon made a garumphing kind of sound deep down in its throat. Fearing the worst, Artos stood and edged toward the jewel and the horrible sword-sized nail that hovered right above it. Leaning over suddenly, he grabbed up the jewel and scuttered back to the cave entrance, breathing loudly.

"I will expect you tomorrow," the dragon said. "You will come during your time off."

Turning, Artos asked over his shoulder, "How do you know I have any?"

"Half an hour after breakfast and two hours at midday and all day every seventh day for the Sabbath, except right before the evening meal," said the dragon.

"But how . . . ?" Artos was astonished because it was true; those *were* the hours he had off.

"When you become as wise as a dragon, you will know these things."

Artos sighed.

"Now listen carefully. There is a quicker path back than the way you came, clambering over the hags and half up to your navel in cold water."

Artos did not ask how the dragon knew about his earlier journey.

"Turn right when you leave the cave and go around the big rock. There is a path straight to the Cowgate. Discover it. And tomorrow, when you come again, you will bring me stew. With *meat!*"

The nail was sheathed with a grinding sound, and the flame from the dragon's hidden mouth flared up one last time as if to light Artos' way out. Then the giant foot withdrew into the darkest part of the cave, clattering as it went.

Just as Artos turned to dash into the light, the wheezy, booming voice came again, filling the cave with echoes.

"Promise, boy. Tooooooooomooooooorow."

"Tomorrow," Artos cried back. "I promise." But he didn't mean a word of it.

3

Home Again

As he hurried from the cave, Artos' mind was a maelstrom of thoughts. Dragon and jewel were topmost of course, swirling about in a red fury. But right below, he worried about the brachet hound in a kind of gray mist. Hidden farther down in the blacker shadows were his anxieties about the long, uncomfortable journey back across the hummocky fens. And beneath it all was the black fear that he'd be punished for staying away so long from his duties. Not once, however, did he reconsider the promise he'd made to the dragon.

Made in haste and under terrible duress, it wasn't the kind of promise one needed to keep.

He tucked the red jewel into the leather bag he wore around his neck on a leather string. The jewel clinked against the little gold ring he kept hidden there, the only keepsake he had from the mother he'd never known.

As it turned out, the journey back was as easy as the dragon had foretold. Somehow Artos hadn't expected that, but his feet found the path—turning naturally where moss and stone had been worn away by years of heavy travel. He wondered briefly why he hadn't come upon it before, but then he remembered that he'd found the cave by clambering up the tor's back side.

The path traversed the fens easily and comfortably, avoiding the wettest places and the cold, meandering stream. He was back within sight of the castle in minutes, feeling only slightly foolish to have been so mistrusting, and also greatly relieved.

Artos grinned broadly at the castle. He was happy to see it but, at the same time, he was amused at its presumption, squatting there in the middle of nowhere. When he'd been younger, he'd thought Sir Ector's *Beau Regarde* a grand place.

21

He could imagine nothing finer. But now, from conversations overheard—if not from any actual experience of other places—he understood how small and unimportant the castle really was. There weren't even any high walls around it, the commonest sign of a castle's power. That was because no one would actually *want* to capture it, or so Cai had said during one of his major pouts. *Beau Regarde* was neither strategically important nor filled with treasure. Just a "small, out-of-the-way, backwater, do-nothing place" Cai had said, groaning, with Bedvere and Lancot agreeing. Still, Artos suddenly realized how much he loved it, how it *suited* him, for he was small and insignificant himself. (*Only now*, his mind reminded him, *we both have a Dragon! So what does small matter?*)

Beau Regarde boasted two large square towers and a splendid gatehouse at the center of the southern entry, as if Sir Ector had begun the place with rather grander plans than he'd finished it with. Or else he'd grown tired of building it halfway through. But it was those towers and gatehouse that Artos was especially fond of. And Lady Marion's garden, with its clipped lawns and the herbaceous border filled with roses blooming till nearly the winter solstice, was Artos' special place to dawdle and dream. He used to climb the high wall between the towers and perch on the parapet (much to Sir Ector's nervous complaints), staring across to the tree-capped horizon. He'd been certain he could see a faraway kingdom. His own kingdom. Where his mother and father waited, grieving for their long lost son. Now, of course, he knew that he had no kingdom. He was a fosterling. And those trees were only a small wood known as Nethy where the best mushrooms grew, for he'd traveled there once with Cook. At Nethy he'd learned that tree trunks weren't always brown, no matter what the poets said. Birch had silver trunks, beech a pewter color, walnuts black, plane trees gray and yellow, and oak trees had trunks that were green with lichen. He was glad to know such things, for he enjoyed knowledge for its own sake, whether it was useful or not.

When he reached the Cowgate he started to run, and he raced into the kennelyard at full tilt because the fear of punishment was suddenly the most real fear of all. As he ran he tried to cobble together five or six alibis, one of which would surely satisfy the Master of Hounds. But surprisingly no one noticed him. Skidding to a stop, he looked around warily, but the Master of Hounds was fast asleep in his great wooden chair, his thin-lipped mouth agape and his long, bandy legs stretched toward the fire. The brachet Boadie lay serene and comfortable by his feet, looking as if she hadn't moved all day.

"You . . . you . . ." Artos whispered at her, but as he couldn't think of a word bad enough to call her, he was silent. She looked up at him then with such certain love in her dark eyes, he knelt down and buried his head into her bulging side. The unborn puppies kicked and squirmed under his cheek and he grinned, fear and anger all forgotten. Boadie smelled so doggy and warm and he was so very tired, he didn't think about dragons anymore but closed his eyes and fell asleep.

Bedvere found him an hour later.

"Slug!" he cried, kicking Artos on the right leg. "Never where you're needed, never where you're supposed to be. Always messing about with dogs and things. Ever a fellow has to search you out. Slug!"

Artos woke with a start and looked up, aggrieved. For a moment he thought of telling Bed about the dragon and showing him the jewel. But only for a moment. Bed would just think the dragon a lie and the jewel stolen. With his slack jaw growing well ahead of the rest of him, Bed looked as unimaginative as he was, and he disliked Artos exactly because Artos *had* an imagination. *No use,* Artos thought, *sharing a dragon with Bed. He'd only want to go and kill it. Kill it! As if that giant clacketing, fire-roaring Master of Wisdoms could be killed by a mere boy.*

It wasn't often that he thought of Bed as a boy, since Bed was fully as large as a man and already had the beginnings of a mustache on his long upper lip. But Artos liked the thought so much, he whispered it to himself again: *mere boy.*

Then, getting to his feet, his right leg still shining with the pain of Bedvere's kick, Artos mumbled, "What do you want, anyway?"

But whatever Bedvere had wanted he'd satisfied with the kick. He'd just come to tell Artos it was time for their supper and was angry at being made a messenger boy for someone he considered well beneath him. Lady Marion had insisted on it and even Bed couldn't refuse to do her wishes, though he didn't have to enjoy it. The message delivered along with the kick, Bedvere was content that he was a messenger boy no longer and left.

Supper was quieter than usual, for Lady Marion was dining with her maids in her chambers and Sir Ector was still out stalking a white deer that had occupied him and his men for the better part of the month. The *Ghost Stag* everyone in the castle called it. Though Sir Ector was a notably poor hunter, he loved nothing better than to be out on the chase with his companions, drinking more than Old Linn, his apothecary-physician, had warned was good for him, and forgetting the manners that Lady Marion insisted upon at home.

The boys made do with a small table by the hearth and told one another lies about their day: comfortable lies, the kind that could be believed honorably. Cai spoke of having almost bested the Master of Swords in one mock battle, Bedvere of having done nearly twenty-seven one-arm push-ups; and Lancot, with his face wreathed in smiles, hinted at having kissed one of Lady Marion's maids, and she all-willing.

The only thing Artos mentioned was the chase after the hound. But when it was clear no one was listening to him, he let the rest of the story dribble away into silence, drinking his well-watered wine with a puckered forehead and an unreadable stare.

Cai rose from the table first. As heir to *Beau Regarde* it was his right.

"Let's play some draughts," he said, stretching his arms wide and looking like a lean, young version of his father.

Bedvere got up and took a carved box out of a great wooden cupboard. He shook it and the game pieces rattled. Lancot took out the playing board. Then the three of them began to play, pointedly ignoring Artos.

The longer he waited for an invitation to join them, the clearer it became that none was forthcoming. He felt his cheeks grow hot, set his lips together, and ground his teeth.

I will not be hurt by them again, he reminded himself, but his hand went up to the leather bag in the unconscious gesture he always made when snubbed by them. The feel of the leather around the little gold ring always comforted him, but this time the bag was heavier and bulkier. He smiled slyly and drew the jewel out, quietly tossing it from palm to palm, hoping one of them would look up from the game and notice.

27

When they didn't, he stuffed the jewel back in the bag and, with little more than an awkward sigh, rose and went out of the room. He thought he heard them laughing as he left, but he couldn't be sure.

The kennelyard was quiet. He wondered if it was Boadie's time yet, but it turned out she was running down the village streets, romping with some of the old hounds Sir Ector hadn't taken with him on the hunt and acting as if she weren't carrying a bellyful of pups. When Artos called to her, she ignored him.

Dreading his dreams, Artos went off to bed.

4

Conversation in the Smithy

The next morning at his break, Artos hurried to the smithy, the jewel clutched in his hand. He was determined to purchase some kind of sword with it, even if it could only buy him a castoff. Though he'd no idea of the jewel's worth, he couldn't wait another moment for the sword. After all, with a sword the other boys would *have* to pay attention to him. He'd be almost a knight.

The jewel in his hand was hard and real and it should have made the whole episode with the dragon seem just as real. Yet somehow it didn't.

The memory of the dragon was vivid enough, but it was the stuff of nightmares: the clacketing scales, the gigantic foot, the keen knifelike nail, the shaft of searing breath flaring hot from the cave's center, the horribly whispery shout. Indeed, he'd dreamed about it all night long. Especially the part about the forced promise to return with meat. Still, only the jewel in his hand, imprinting itself on his palm, seemed real. The reality of the dragon and the promise were carefully buried under layers of small-boy caution and years of polished imaginings. He would have been perfectly satisfied to leave them in the land of never-was, but then he arrived at the smithy in the middle of a quarrel.

The quarrel was between Sir Ector's apothecary Old Linn and Magnus Pieter the swordmaker. It was a whiney, word-whipping sort of argument that—because it isn't shouted—you don't realize it's happening until you're right in the middle of it and can't possibly escape. Artos had thought it an ordinary conversation until he was inside the smithy door, and then it was too late because the two of them looked over and saw him and he couldn't leave without embarrassment and loss of face to one or the other.

They noticed him but, in the manner of adults, they didn't stop arguing. It was as if his presence added fuel to their fires, as if each were trying to impress him so that he might choose up sides.

"But there's never any *meat* in my gravy," Old Linn was saying, his voice rising into a mealy whine at the end. It was the word *meat* spoken in that way that brought the dragon's last words back to Artos. *Meat in the stew* was what the dragon wanted and what Artos had promised. He shivered.

"Nor any meat in your manner," replied the smith. "Nor do you mete out punishment." He fancied himself quite a wordsmith as well as a swordsmith, and so stated to any castle newcomers.

In fact, Magnus Pieter was not much good with words, being a lumbering sort of person. He was really only comfortable with iron and fire and the great bellows in the smithy. It was well known that he rehearsed his word jokes, banging them out with each fall of the hammer onto the anvil. Artos could almost hear the rehearsal for this rain of puns: "*Meat* in the gravy (*bang*), *meat* in your manner (*bang*), *mete* out punishment (*bang*), *meet* you in battle (*bang*)."

31

Once upon a time, Magnus Pieter had been regularly spitted in public by Old Linn's quick tongue. They'd been best friends by their long and rancorous association. But last year Old Linn had had a fit, brought on Cook said "by age and all them secrets of his." He'd fallen face first into his bowl of soup during one of the High King's infrequent visits to the castle. And now Magnus Pieter was the castle wit ("What,—*bang!*—the wit—*bang!*") and Old Linn a shambling wreck of an old man who never stood up after meals to tell any more of the great tales. Artos had loved the few stories he'd been allowed to stay up for.

Old Linn hunched around the forge looking more like a tortoise than a man, his thin shoulders bent over as if they wore a carapace instead of a tunic, his scrawny neck poking out between the humps. His eyes were rheumy and staring. *Definitely a tortoise*, Artos thought.

"My straw is never changed but once a se'ennight," Old Linn whined. "My slops are never emptied. I am given but the dregs of the wine to drink. And now I must sit—if I am welcomed at all—well below the salt."

Well below the salt. Artos knew full well the sting of that, for being seated below the salt meant to be in a place of no honor at all at the table. To sit alongside the impoverished and the nameless, like himself. Only it wasn't exactly true. Old Linn had never sat by him, but rather at the High Table not far from Lady Marion. He wondered why Old Linn bothered to lie about it. It was only later, after he'd left the smithy, that he understood the old man was exaggerating, as storytellers always do, for the effect.

The smith smiled but never stopped the tap-tap-tapping on the piece of iron he was working. He argued back to the beat of the hammer. "But you've got straw (*bang*), though you no longer earn it (*bang*). And a pot for your slops (*bang*), which you could empty yourself (*bang*). You've got wine (*bang bang*), though you never pay for it (*blow bellows*). And even below the salt there's gravy in the bowls (*turn over iron, bang-bang-bang*)."

Artos nodded at that because he knew there *was* gravy in the bowls, even when you sat well below the salt. Sir Ector was a kind man and Lady Marion insisted on it. Then, realizing the nod had suddenly brought him right into the middle of their conversation when he hadn't meant to be in it at all, he instantly regretted that nod.

But they ignored him anyway, and Old Linn repeated his piteous whine.

"But there is never any *meat* in my gravy."

At the word *meat*, Magnus Pieter was off again,
beating out five or six slightly new variations on
the anvil, and this time the word rang like a knell
in Artos' head. The hammer sounded like the
clanking dragon scales and the word *meat* was
spoken each time as the dragon had spoken it:
loud, commanding, and with great implied mean-
ing.

Artos swallowed back all his own saved-up
words. Clutching the jewel so tightly it left a
deep print in his palm, he slunk out of the smithy.
He'd never even had a chance to mention the
sword, that shining piece of steel that might have
made him the equal of any of the castle boys.
And what good anyway, he thought miserably,
*is the dragon's wisdom or the dragon's jewel to
me? Or the dragon?*

5

The Getting of Wisdom

Artos struggled all the rest of the morning with his promise. Yet—though he couldn't quite put into words why—he found himself in the kitchen begging a pot of gravy with meat at the beginning of his two-hour break. He would have been happier asking Cook herself, but she was sleeping off the heavy noon meal of soup, beef, and turnips. It was to Mag the scullery, hard at work scouring out the great tureens, whom he had to do his pleading.

Mag was his bane. Several years his senior,

she was small, wiry, and always smelled of garlic, with a bristly dark mustache like a scar under her nose. She'd had an unlikely passion for him ever since he was a small boy. While all the other serving girls moped after Lancot with his gold curls and maddening smiles, Mag longed for Artos. He gritted his teeth and spoke directly into the middle of her sighs.

"Mag, could I get another pot of gravy with meat?"

She sighed. "Master Artos, what would you be needing a pot for? (*Sigh*) Not for that scamp, Boadie? (*Sigh*) She's big as a tun already. (*Sigh*)"

"No, not for any dog," he said quickly.

She waited expectantly for the rest of the answer.

"For . . . for . . . for . . ." Now when he most needed it, once again his imagination failed him.

"For yourself, Master Artos? (*Sigh*) I'd gladly give it . . . thee. (*Sigh*)"

The *thee*, familiar and tender, was so daring on her part that he grabbed for it at once.

"Yes, for myself. For me."

"Thee. And growing into thy full manhood (*Sigh*) and needing such sustenance. (*Sigh*)" She actually fluttered her eyelashes at him in a terrible imitation of one of Lady Marion's maids, adding slyly, "And what'll thee give a poor girl for it? (*Sigh.*)"

"Give?" He hadn't considered the need of any exchange. Gulping, he managed to whisper, "My thanks, Mag?" He hoped it was enough.

In the end it hadn't been enough. Mag was a crafty bargainer. He'd had to kiss her on the cheek, avoiding the stink of garlic by the simple expedient of holding his breath. He kissed her between one deep sigh and the next and escaped with the pot of gravy lumped with three pieces of meat.

Artos strolled casually out of the Cowgate as if he had all the time in the world, nodding slightly at the sleepy-looking guards standing over the portcullis. Overhead a marsh harrier coursed the sky.

Artos could feel his heartbeat quicken and he went faster across the moat bridge, glancing briefly at the gray-green water where the ancient moat tortoise—looking remarkably like Old Linn—lazed atop the rusted crown of a battle helm. Once he was across, he began to run.

As he ran, it occurred to him that if the dragon

wanted more stew—in fact stew every day—he might have to give Mag more kisses. Kisses on the cheek and, perhaps, kisses right on her garlicky mouth. He wrinkled his nose at the thought. This business of dragons could very quickly get out of hand.

Since kissing Mag didn't bear thinking about, he concentrated instead on the path. Though he hadn't noticed in his haste to get home the day before, it was a quite well-worn thread, winding through the wilderness of peat mosses and tangled brush, past bright yellow kingcup and the white clusters of milk parsley. Once he had to clamber over two rock outcroppings that looked rather like the lumps of meat, and once he had to free his hose from a briar. But they were little troubles compared to the peat pools farther north that everyone knew held bones way far down, and only the fen folk could traverse safely day after day on their hidden paths.

He got to the cave much quicker than he'd bargained. Breathless and unprepared (*Indeed, how does one prepare for a dragon?* he thought), he squinted nervously into the dark hole. It was much less inviting than yesterday. He listened hard but this time heard none of the heavy dragon breathing.

"Perhaps," he said aloud to lend himself courage, "perhaps there's no one at home. Perhaps I can just leave the pot of gravy and go."

"STAAAAAAAY," came the sudden rumbling. Artos almost dropped the pot.

"I . . . I have the gravy," he shouted. He hadn't meant to speak so loudly, but fear always made him either too quiet or too loud, and he was never sure which it was going to be.

"Then give it meeeeeeee," said the voice, somewhat modulated and followed immediately by a clanking as the great claw extended halfway through the cave.

Artos could tell it was the foot by its long shadow, for this time there was no illuminating gout of fire. There was only a hazy smoldering from the far end of the cave. All of a sudden—things seeming fairly familiar—Artos felt a little braver. "I shall need to take the pot back with me. When you are quite done with it. Sir."

"You shall take a bit of wisdom instead," the dragon said.

"Please, sir, I'd rather have the pot." But fear

had made his voice so quiet, he could hardly hear it himself. At the same time, he wondered if the dragon's wisdom would make him wise enough to avoid Mag's garlicky embrace. Somehow he doubted it was *that* kind of wisdom.

"Tomorrow you shall have the pot," the dragon said. "When you bring me more meat."

"More?" This time Artos' voice squeaked unaccountably. He could already smell Mag.

"MOOOOOOOORE." The nail on the dragon's foot extended just as it had the day before, catching under the handle of the pot. There was a hideous screeching as the pot was lifted several inches into the air and slowly withdrawn into the recesses of the cave. Then came strange scrabbling noises, as if the dragon were sorting through its various possessions, before the clanking resumed. When the claw returned, it dropped something at Artos' feet.

He looked down. It was a book, rather tatty around the edges. The cave light was so dim, he couldn't read its title.

"Wissssssssdom," hissed the dragon alarmingly, like a kettle almost out of water yet still on the boil.

Artos shrugged. "It's just a book. And anyway,

I already know my letters. Father Bertram taught me."

"Letterssssss turn matter into ssssspirit."

"You mean it's a book of magic?"

"All books are magic, boy." The dragon sounded a bit cranky and that made Artos begin to get very nervous again.

"Well, I can read," Artos said quickly, hoping to soothe the agitated beast. He stooped and picked up the book, very much aware of the claw near his head. Then, looking hopefully in the dragon's direction and trying to pierce the darkness and read the dragon's expression, he said, "Thank you." *Old thorns and old dragons*, he reminded himself.

"You can read *letters*, my boy, which is more than I can say for your thick-headed castle contemporaries. And you can read *words*. But in order to gain wisdom you must learn to read *inter linea*, between the lines."

Edging backward toward the light of the cave entrance, but not so quickly as to alert the dragon, Artos opened the book and scanned the first page. His fingers underlined each word while his mouth formed them aloud. He turned the page, then looked up puzzled. "You must have given me a damaged book, sir. There is nothing written between the lines."

Something rather like a chuckle crossed with a cough echoed around the cave. The dragon was laughing.

"There is always something written between the lines, boy, but it takes great wisdom to read it."

"Then why me, sir? As you have already noted, I have very little wisdom." He added uncertainly, afraid he might have issued an invitation to eating, "In fact, sir, I am very little all over."

"Because . . . because you are here."

"Here?"

"Today. And not back at *Beau Regarde* feeding the brachets or cleaning out the mews or sweating in the smithy or cowering before that pack of unruly, bulky, illiterate boys. You are here, Artos. For the getting of wisdom." The dragon made stretching noises.

"Oh!" It was a temporizing sound. He'd originally thought that coming back to the cave was a mistake. Now he was beginning to wonder what had really brought him. Not fear of the dragon, surely. As long as the dragon was in a cave and he'd been at the castle, there was nothing to fear. Or so he thought. Could he *really* have come back to get the wisdom the dragon had promised? He liked *knowing* things, and *knowing* was certainly a part of wisdom. But at least Father Bertram wouldn't eat him if he missed a word. The dragon might. The getting of wisdom from dragons could be a very dangerous game.

There was a sudden tremendous wheezing and clanking and a strange *Uh-oh* from the dragon. Then silence.

Artos peered nervously at the back of the cave. He could see nothing but blackness streaked with an occasional quick finger of fire. The silence lasted a long, long time. Finally Artos ventured, "Are you all right, sir?"

An even longer silence followed in which he began to wonder if he should make his way through that awful blackness to the back of the cave. He wondered if this were another test and if he had enough courage to pierce that darkness. And he wondered if he had even the smallest amount of the wisdom necessary to help out if something really were wrong with the dragon. Then, just as he was about to try, the dragon's voice came hissing back.

"Yessssssssss, boy."

"Yes, what, sir?" He'd forgotten the question in his nervousness.

"Yesssssss, I'm all right."

"Well then," Artos said, putting one foot quietly behind another, "thank you for my wisdom and I'll be going, sir."

A furious flame spat across the cave, leaping through the darkness to lick Artos' feet. He jumped back, startled at the dragon's accuracy and suddenly terribly afraid. Had it all just been preparation for the dragon's dinner? Did the dragon season his prey with anticipation and fear? Had the stew gravy with the three lumps of meat been a small appetizer before the main course, which was to be an Artos roasted slowly on that gleaming nail over the dragon's own fiery flames? Artos' imagination worked double time, and he could already feel the searing agony of the fire, could already smell his flesh burning, could already hear the sizzling of his hair. Suddenly he wished above all things that he'd stayed at the smithy, waiting out the argument between Old Linn and Magnus Pieter to claim a sword. Any sword. Even a full-on-the-mouth kiss from Mag would be preferable to being a dragon's dinner. If he got out of this, he promised himself to be nicer to Mag in the future. Taking a deep breath, he turned and ran out of the cave.

Only the dragon's voice followed him.

"Sssssssilly child, that was not the wisdom."

From a safe place outside the cave, Artos called out. "There's more?"

"By the time I am through with you, Artos Pendragon, Arthur son of the dragon, you will read *inter linea* in people as well." There was a loud moan and another round of furious clacketing, and then total silence.

Taking the silence as a dismissal, and clutching the book hard against his chest, Artos ran down the hill. *Artos Pendragon.* Why ever had the dragon called him that? He worried *that* particular bit of dragon wisdom over and over until the castle was in sight. After that, he'd only one thought in mind: *What can I tell Mag about the loss of the gravy pot?* It might mean another kiss. Actually, the dragon's fires would have been preferable. And, comfortably forgetting his promise to be nicer to Mag, he ran all the way back home.

6

The Getting of a Sword

The minute he was back in the castle, Artos found a quiet corner and opened the book. He looked at it grimly, turning page after page. There were no pictures in it, only writing; and it was immediately clear he wouldn't be able to read it without help. The sentences were much too long and interspersed with Latin and other tongues whose letters were totally foreign to him. He could only guess at their meanings. He wondered if that were the *between the lines* the dragon had meant.

Closing the book with a bang—which caused

a great amount of dust to get up his nose, tickling him into three mighty sneezes—Artos was filled with disappointment. After all his courage in facing the dragon again *and* the kiss he'd bravely given to Mag, the least he'd expected was the promised wisdom. So much for promises!

He couldn't ask Father Bertram for help in reading it. The priest (*prickly as an old thorn bush,* he thought) would never approve of any book other than the Testament or commentaries. The good father was fierce about what he considered proper fare for Christians, especially new Christians like the castle folk, still prone to backsliding. Artos remembered the great bonfires when Father Bertram had first arrived, into which the priest had personally flung book after book. Even Lady Marion's *Book of Hours*, with its gold leafing and colored miniatures, a gift from the High King that had taken some four scribes the better part of a year to set down, even that had gone into Father Bertram's righteous flames. And Lady Marion, who'd insisted they all become Christians in the first place, could not argue. Rumor had it that the book was burned because Adam and Eve wore no fig leaves and there weren't any scribes in such a small place as *Beau Regarde* who might paint them in. Artos smiled at the thought. He wished he'd seen the pictures before the flames had gotten to it. In the interest of wisdom, of course.

He'd seen neither the *Book of Hours* nor the flames to which it had been consigned, but he'd had the story on good authority when, some years later, Lady Marion had sighed in mentioning it to her maids and they passed the sigh along with the gravy down to young Cai, who'd mentioned it as a joke to Bed and Lancot in the cowshed where Artos, unbeknownst to them, was trying to nap in the haymow.

No, he couldn't ask Father Bertram for help in reading the dragon's book. Pictures or no, he doubted the dragon's wisdom was the same as the good father's and another book would be consigned to the fire. His only recourse, he knew with a slow, sinking feeling, was to ask Old Linn, that whiney, hunched-over, ancient embarrassment. He'd have to wait until suppertime of course, after the rest of his chores. Then he'd make an appointment with the old man, out of the hearing of the other boys; an appointment to visit Old Linn in his tower room.

At the thought of the tower room, Artos shivered. He'd never been up there. None of the boys had. It was rumored to be filled with bottles of poison and beakers of strange-colored liquids. The door itself, so he'd heard, was set about with runic warnings and enchantments.

But Old Linn was his only hope, tower room or no. The apothecary could read four languages well—English, Latin, Greek, and bardic runes. It was said his room was piled floor to ceiling with books, the only ones Father Bertram hadn't been able to burn because the old man wasn't a Christian. Old Linn had known great stories, many of them from those very books, like "The Conception of Pryderi" and "The Battle of the Trees" and the ones about the children of Llyr and the Cauldron and the Iron House and the horse for Bran. Artos suddenly wished he'd had one of *those* books instead of the dragon's useless book of wisdom. Especially since Old Linn was now too enfeebled to recite the tales.

Artos hoped, sincerely, that the apothecary was at least well enough to help him read the dragon's book but not well enough to ask him how he'd secreted such a treasure away from Father Bertram's fires. If asked, he'd say it was a present from his mother. Unconsciously, his hand strayed to the leather bag around his neck. *Yes,* he thought, *old men are often sentimental. He'll believe that.* Then he added, quickly, *I hope.*

Of course, there *was* a further problem. Artos knew that Old Linn hated him. Well, perhaps *hate* was too strong a word, but he certainly preferred the other young gentlemen of *Beau Regarde*—the heir Cai and his two cousins Bedvere and Lancot. Preferred them to the impoverished fosterling who'd been taken in as an infant by the kindness of Sir Ector and the tenderness of Lady Marion. The old man especially lavished attention on Cai who, as far as Artos was concerned, had long ago let his muscles overtake his head. And Bed, whose hand was as heavy as his long jaw. And that pretty boy Lancot. Even though they were all—and here he recalled the dragon's words with pleasure—*unruly, bulky, illiterate boys.*

Once, of course, he'd tried desperately to curry favor with them, fetching and carrying and helping them with their letters. But after Lancot, as a joke, had pulled Artos' hose and pants down around his ankles in the courtyard and the other two—with great gasps of laughter—had called out Lady Marion's maids to gawk, Artos had tried to ignore them whenever possible. Or had tried to make them ask him for help, which happened all too rarely.

Still, whether Old Linn hated him or preferred the others, it didn't matter. Surely the getting of wisdom was a time for putting aside feelings of hurt. He'd need a lot of help in reading the dragon's book. And since none of the other boys could read even half as well as he and Sir Ector couldn't read at all and Lady Marion must never know about such frightening things as dragons and Father Bertram would burn his book, Old Linn was his only hope.

As Artos grimly climbed the stairs to the tower, the book weighed heavily under his arm. He rehearsed his speech at each step.

"Old Linn," he whispered to himself. "Sir Linn." *That was better.* "I feel a great need at this time in my life to get wisdom and . . ." *Would he believe that?* "I met this dragon the other day and he thought I needed to . . ." *No, best keep the dragon secret. After all, old dragons like old thorns . . .* "I came upon this book and . . ." *Surely Old Linn would know the list of books left over from the Father Bertram's fires. It was no good. Each step closer to the tower room made the excuses seem feebler.*

There were 113 steps in all. Artos counted them between speeches. 113. A magical-sounding number. The last few steps he had to take in utter darkness because the torch at the top of the stairs by the door had guttered out. When he touched it, he found it so cold he knew it had been dead for hours.

Because of the darkness, he couldn't see the many runes on the door. Indeed, he couldn't see the door, only feel its hard wood under his hand. He found a great metal knocker by feel as well and used it to tap lightly on the door.

When there was no answer, he hammered more loudly.

After thirteen loud knocks (*Another magical number*, he told himself), he knew there was no one inside. He couldn't tell if he were unhappy or immeasurably relieved. Trotting down the stairs, he was too late for dinner and too upset to be hungry. So, chancing a whipping by ignoring his after-dinner duties, he went instead to speak to Old Linn's best friend, the smith.

"Come now, young Art," the smith called out. "And wasn't you here just this morning with a grim and gruesome look? What is't?"

Artos smiled, all the while trying to think of a way to introduce Old Linn seamlessly into the conversation, but failing.

"Shouldn't you be at work, boy? Shouldn't I?" asked the smith. "The ayes (*bang*) have it," he said, turning back to his anvil and starting out on another round of word jokes.

In order to stop the jokes and, partially because it seemed as good a time as ever, Artos reached up and took the leather bag from around his neck. He fingered it open and drew out the red jewel, dropping it onto the anvil, where it made a funny little pinging sound.

Magnus Pieter sucked on his lower lip and snorted solemnly through his nose. "God's truth, boy—where'd you get that stone?" He let the hammer down slowly till it rested by his boot.

To tell the truth would mean getting swat for a liar, that much Artos knew. So he borrowed the lie he'd prepared to tell Old Linn who was, at any rate, a great deal sharper than the smith.

"I was left it by my mother. Same as this ring."

He lifted out the little golden circle, which could only rest on the tip part of his pinkie, being so tiny and perfect. The lie, using his unknown mother as a base, sat uneasily in his mouth. He was, by inclination, an honest boy though his imagination sometimes led him into a storyteller's exaggerations. But the smith didn't seem to notice.

"Kept it till now, have you?" Magnus Pieter asked. "Well, well, and of course you have. There's not much in *Beau Regarde* to spend such a fine jewel on."

"Is it fine then?" asked Artos quietly. Up until then he'd no idea if the jewel were real or only colored glass.

Magnus Pieter nodded, his head moving up and down several times. "Very fine."

Artos found himself nodding back, the silence between them stretching their agreement.

At last Magnus Pieter could stand no more silence. "And why'd you be showing this special jewel to Old Magpie, eh?" It was the boys' name for him, and Artos was surprised he knew it. "Because you know I'd appreciate fine craft?" He spoke with the heavy-handed jocularity he always confused with cunning.

Guessing the smith would give him a better

bargain if he played the innocent, Artos replied simply, "Why, I thought I might buy a sword, Magnus Pieter."

"Of course," the smith said, throwing his head back and bellowing a laugh. "A sword!" Then he stopped and cocked his head to one side, eyeing Artos and, Artos thought, looking very much like a large magpie indeed. "Well?"

"Well, I am old enough now to have a sword of my own," Artos said. "And if the jewel from my . . . mother . . ."—his voice dropped suddenly at the lie—"is as fine as you say, perhaps I can buy a *good* sword, too."

"As fine as I say—you say—but I be no great judge of jewels."

"But a judge of swords," said Artos, adding in a whisper, "and words." The last felt like the worst lie of all, which is why he whispered it, but it appealed greatly to Magnus Pieter, whose chest positively swelled.

"A swordsmith and a wordsmith, true," said the smith. Grinning, he added, "How good a sword might you like, boy?"

Artos knelt down beside the anvil and the red jewel was then at the level of his eyes. As if he were addressing the stone and not the smith, he chanted a bit from a song that Old Linn used to sing:

"And aye their swords soe sore can byte,
Through help of gramarye . . ."

Magnus Pieter looked around quickly. "Best you not let Father Bertram hear you sing that, young Art." He sighed. "But I know when I must do what must be done. I been warned, I have. I've got the signs. So I'll make you a fine sword, a steel of power. And while I make it, you must think of a name for your sword. A sword bought with a fine stone. A sword from a stone, boy. So it goes. So it goes. There will be history in it." He reached across the anvil and plucked up the jewel, holding it high over both their heads.

Artos stood slowly, never once taking his eyes from the jewel, but wondering all the while what the smith had been jabbering about. *Old men,* he thought, *and their strange sentiments, signs, and portents.* For a moment he thought he saw dragon fire leaping and crackling across the jewel's surface, reflecting from the jewel's core. Then he realized it was merely mirroring the glowing coals of the forge.

"Perhaps," he said, thinking out loud, "perhaps

I will call my sword *Inter Linea*."

The smith smiled. "A fine name, that. Makes me think of foreign climes." He pocketed the jewel and began to work, his hammer banging out another chain of jokes around the word *clime*.

Artos ran out, heading toward the mews where he knew he'd at least several hours of work helping out the Master of Hawks. It was a job he hated with a passion, as the birds all seemed so desolate to him, standing about on their perches and jangling their jesses when they'd rather be out cresting the currents of air.

7

Days of Wisdom

If he wanted a pot of stew, it would mean another slobbery kiss from Mag. Artos knew this and, at last, accepted it. He'd come to understand that wisdom was not to be gotten easily.

Fortunately, Mag was content with kisses on the cheek, gathering them in with such blushes and sighs that Artos found himself embarrassed for her, not appalled by her. It was rather sad, really, how little she was willing to settle for. He thought: *When I have my wisdom, perhaps I can give Mag some.*

The walk to the dragon's cave, first taken by accident, then in fear, became something Artos looked forward to each day with positive delight. He still stole out of the Cowgate carefully, unwilling to share the dragon's whereabouts with any of the boys. But he didn't care if the guards at the back gate noticed him. If they did, they could hardly guess his destination. One or another usually waved him on, then turned back sleepily to chat with a companion. They were, Artos knew, guards in name only. Sir Ector's *Beau Regarde* really *was* a little place, as small and as insignificant as Cai had always made it out to be. This much wisdom he'd already gained from his time with the dragon.

The dragon had spoken knowingly of other lands, lands that Artos was sure it had flown over while hunting for a proper cave of its own.

"The world is round like an apple," the dragon had said, "and so in the Far East, which is on the bottom side of the world from us, are the Indies where men walk upon their hands instead of their feet."

Artos had tried that when he returned to the kennelyard, but only succeeded in wrenching his shoulder so badly he was of no use to the Master of Hounds when later that afternoon Boadie gave birth to a litter of nine pups.

Another day the dragon had informed him, "In Jerusalem, where the Pilate washed his hands of your Jesus, men wear dresses and turbans and have faces as black as mud."

Artos had examined his own face carefully that evening in a bowl of scented water. But even in the flickering candlelight, his face was as pale as the milk Boadie's pups licked so eagerly. He thought he could love a friend with a face the color of rich earth, so different from his own.

Each day the dragon doled out its wisdoms, sometimes from the book it had given Artos and sometimes letting him read from other books bound in leathers as variegated as a summer posy, with illuminations in cinnabar, rubric, cobalt blue, and daffodil gold. And sometimes it dropped the books onto the cave floor and simply spun him tales, golden threads of story that wove inevitably into a tapestry of knowledge. He heard about lands beneath the sea, drowned cities where the bells of churches still sounded with each passing wave; about lands where stone beasts with the faces of women ruled over the desert sands; about lands where men could ride on woven carpets high in the temperate air; about a land where a king might hold together a group of unruly knights by the simple magic of making them sit at a round table where no one was below the salt, where no one was higher, where all could be equal in the sight of their lord.

The dragon sometimes sang him ballads, too, in a voice made soft by music. He sang songs from the prickly, heather-covered lands of the Scots who ran naked and screaming into battle; and sagas from the cold, icy Norsemen who prowled the coasts in their dragon-prowed ships; and songs of love from the silk-and-honey lands of Araby.

It even told him riddles and their answers, like:

As round as an apple, as deep as a cup,
And all the king's horses can't pull it up

which Artos guessed as "a well," correctly as it turned out, so wise he was becoming.

The best day, though, was the sunny spring day when he ran all the way with *four* lumps of

meat in the pot (Mag had been especially suscepti-
ble to his kiss) to be greeted by a jolly "Halloooooo,
Artos!"

"Halloooooo, sir," he called back. "Four lumps
of meat, not three!"

There was a chuckling from the inner cave.
"And I have something particular for you as well,
my boy."

With an especially loud clanking and creaking,
a noise that now seemed so comfortably familiar
Artos scarcely heard it anymore, the dragon
pushed forward three pots, the one from the day
before and two it must have secreted in its hoard.
All three pots were exactly alike. Carefully the
foot chose out a very large green jewel from the
cave floor.

"An emerald," said the dragon. "Do you know
it?"

"An emerald," repeated Artos, who by now had
discovered that if he repeated anything the dragon
taught him two or three times, he never forgot
it. "An emerald."

"There are those who say emeralds have an
evil temperament, but I have always thought them
one of the most beautiful jewels in the world.
What do you think, boy?"

Artos considered the jewel by the flickering light of the dragon's breath.

"An emerald," he said thoughtfully, the word now fully his. "Grass is as green, and new leaves, and the hills all glowing in early spring. Green has always seemed to me one of God's favorite colors."

The dragon was silent. It was usually a sign that he was pleased with Artos' answer. A wrong answer always brought a swift correction.

Encouraged by the silence, Artos continued, "So I think a jewel that is green cannot be evil at all. Not on this world, anyway."

The dragon chuckled fondly at him, a strange *chu-chu-chu* sound. "Now I will give you this lovely green jewel to keep for your very own if you can find it under the right pot." It placed the emerald carefully under one of the pots and began to mix the pots around.

Leaning forward on his stone seat, Artos concentrated with all his will. He didn't really want the jewel as much as he wanted to make the dragon proud of him.

Round and round the pots went, until Artos was almost dizzy with them. Then the clacketing of the dragon's leg slowed and, at last, stopped.

"Do you know which pot the jewel lies under?" the dragon asked.

"That one," he said, pointing confidently.

The dragon lifted the pot he'd indicated. The jewel was not there.

"It *has* to be," Artos said. "I never took my eye off it."

"But it is not," the dragon said. "Watch again. I will still give you the jewel if you guess the right pot this time."

Artos watched again as the pots circled. The dragon used two feet this time, not one, and the extra clatter was loud in the cave, but Artos was never distracted. When the dragon stopped moving the pots around, Artos said nothing but pointed, to the *correct* pot this time.

When the dragon lifted it up, there was nothing underneath.

Angrily, Artos leaned forward and picked up the other two pots. The emerald was not under any of them.

Chuckling loudly, the dragon turned over its claw. The emerald was firmly tucked into the deep sharp creases of the palm.

"That's a cheat!" Artos cried petulantly.

"Will you watch again?"

"NO!"

But he did, not once but many times, though he could never catch the dragon palming the green jewel. At last he sat back.

"What wisdom is this, O Master of Riddles?"

"It is many different wisdoms," the dragon said, "but you shall have to figure them out for yourself."

Then he taught Artos exactly how the game was played.

Artos went back to the castle, having practiced the game of pot and jewel for over an hour till he got it right. He refused the emerald when the dragon offered it, saying, "I didn't guess the right pot, so I've no right to the jewel."

The dragon had snorted, then answered, "But there wasn't any *right* pot."

Still, Artos wouldn't take it, and felt marvelously righteous and impoverished as he trotted home. It was a wonderful feeling.

Even better was the feeling he got after supper when, borrowing three identical cups from the table and using a rather large pea he'd saved out, he fooled Cai, Lancot, and Bed. They even bet coins on the outcome and lost seven times in a row. It made for a handsome pile of coins.

That's when Cai had threatened him and Artos, grandly and with great apparent pleasure, pushed the coins back across the table toward Cai saying, "If the future lord of *Beau Regarde* insists . . ."

Lancot had put his hand over Cai's before he could pick up the coppers.

"He beat you fairly, Cai," Lancot said.

Bedvere had grunted his grudging agreement.

Straightening up and looking sourly across the table at Artos, Cai had left the coins.

Fairly. The word rankled. All at once the good feeling was gone. Artos wondered if he *had* beaten Cai fairly. Was tricking someone the same as beating him? What if that someone were bigger and older and higher in rank—was it all right to cheat then? Or what, he wondered suddenly, if it were the other way around. Was it all right to trick someone like Mag, someone insignificant and worthless and way down the ranks? And—the traitor thought insisted on winding into his brain— was *anyone* that insignificant, that worthless?

He felt all out of sorts at the questions. None of them seemed to have easy answers.

It was when he was almost asleep, lying comfortably in the featherbed, that he knew that this idea of *fairness* was at least one of the wisdoms to be gotten from the dragon's game.

But the dragon had said there were many different wisdoms therein. He wondered, right before sleep claimed him, if wisdom itself was the jewel under the cup. Not really there at all. He dreamed about jewels and cups and dragons far, far into the night.

8

Day of the Sword

All the while Artos was trotting back and forth
to the dragon's cave gaining his wisdom, Magnus
Pieter was fast at work on the sword. But he
didn't get it right, not at first. Each new steel
had something wrong with it, and Artos refused
each in turn.

"I don't have this much trouble with Sir Ector
himself, I don't," complained the smith, forgetting
in his grousing to beat out any new jokes on the
anvil.

"But the hilt doesn't sit comfortably in my

hand," Arthur said of the first sword. That hilt, artfully shaped like two entwined serpents, was in fact much too big for him. But even if it had been smaller, he wouldn't have wanted it. He had a horror of serpents.

"Ah, well, Sir Bedvere is needing a new blade. He snapped his last trying to beat a tree in fair combat," said Magnus Pieter with a gruff laugh. "Snakes is just for him."

The smith was right, of course, and so pleased with the coins Bed gave him for the sword (snakes were *just* the thing and Bed insisted on being called "Serpent's Bane" by everyone for weeks), it was a month before Magnus Pieter felt the need to work on another sword, catching up instead on his horseshoeing and a special order from Lady Marion for a new candelabrum.

The second sword had a strange crossbar on it that the smith insisted would protect the hand.

"It's my own invention!" he said, pride getting well in the way of any jokes.

Privately Artos thought the thing unbalanced, but aloud only said he wouldn't have it.

"You *are* a priss," the smith said sourly. "It's not as if it's to be your last sword ever."

"But it *is* to be my first sword ever," Artos answered quietly. "And you *did* say it was a very fine jewel."

Magnus Pieter growled and shook his head, but as he'd already set the jewel in a sword hilt for Sir Ector and Artos knew it and Magnus Pieter knew he knew it, he couldn't very well give the jewel back.

"Besides, you know how Cai prizes newness above all things," Artos said, a bit of wisdom the dragon had shared with him just that week when talking about the importance of balancing the old and the new. "I would think he'd give you a gold coin to have the first sword ever made with that kind of hilt."

Grinning, Magnus Pieter turned back to the forge. He raised his hammer and began to beat out a piece of steel, saying, "I *knew* (*bang*) and you *knew* (*bang*) that Cai loves the very *new* (*bang*) and . . ."

Artos made his escape quickly, still swordless. He guessed it would be more weeks yet before the smith began *anew* (*bang*). He'd probably spend the next weeks fashioning plowshares and door latches and forks and hoes.

The third sword was still bright from its tempering, with a lovely pattern running down the blade, when Lancot claimed it. Artos didn't even have a chance to try. He came into the smithy just as Lancot was slicing the air with the steel.

"Cai and Bed have new swords," Lancot was saying, "and I want this."

Before Artos could complain, Old Linn hobbled in. It had been quite a while since Artos had seen the apothecary. He'd decided not to seek out the old man but rather to puzzle through the dragon's book on his own, and had been delighted to find he'd some skill at deciphering the Latin after all. But he was shocked at Old Linn's appearance. His mouth and hair were yellowed with a lingering illness and his hands trembled. Still, when he spoke, his voice had its old strength, with none of the whine about it.

"You were always a man true to his word," Old Linn reminded the smith.

"And true to my swords," Magnus Pieter replied, seemingly delighted to be playing with his old friend again.

"That sword was promised elsewhere," Old Linn said. *"Remember!"*

Artos bit his lip, wondering how the old man had known, then smiled. Of course. Magnus Pieter would have told him.

The smith looked down at his hands and Artos was surprised to see them trembling fully as much as the apothecary's. Taking his cue, Artos stepped from the shadows and held out his own hand. The smith took the sword from Lancot and gave it to Artos, who turned it this way and that to catch the light. The watering on the blade made a pattern that looked a great deal like the flames from a dragon's mouth. It sat well and balanced in his hand, feeling like an extension of his own arm. When he sliced it through the air, the sword actually hummed, a note he could feel straight through to his heart.

"He likes the blade," said Old Linn. "So it was meant."

Magnus Pieter shrugged and hid his hands behind him.

Artos gave the sword a few more cuts through the air just to feel that note again. When he turned to thank the apothecary, the old man was gone. So was Lancot. He could see them through the smithy door, walking arm and arm up the castle wynd.

"So, you've got your *Inter Linea* now," said Magnus Pieter. "And about time you chose one. There was nothing wrong with them other two."

"You got good prices for them," Artos reminded him.

The smith turned back to his anvil, the clang of hammer on steel ending their conversation.

At his long break, Artos ran out of the castle by the Cowgate, halloing so loudly and waving the sword with such vigor that the guards laughed and pointed at him. Even the ancient tortoise dozing on the rusted helm lifted its sleepy head for a moment. Overhead a lapwing and a golden plover crossed the roads of air. Artos lifted his face to the sky, a kind of pagan thanks.

Holding the sword with two hands, he fairly leaped over the two lumpy rocks in the path. He recalled one of the stories the dragon had told him—of the wild, naked Scots. For a moment as he leaped, he pretended he was one of them—a Douglas or a MacGregor. Landing on his knees, he did a forward roll and then stood up, the sword still before him. *A naked Scot*, he thought with a smile, *would have gotten terribly bruised with that maneuver.* He was suddenly thankful for his jerkin and hose.

At the cave entrance, he brushed himself off carefully. Then, hefting the sword, he called out as he walked in.

"Ho! Old flame tongue." The sword seemed to allow him a certain familiarity he'd never attempted with the dragon before. "Furnace lung, look what I've got. My sword. From that jewel you gave me. Magnus Pieter called it a sword from a stone and got all silly about it. And he had to try three times before he made what I wanted. He almost didn't give it to me until Old Linn came in, shaking like an autumn tree, and reminded him of his promise. Come see. It's a rare beauty and I'm going to call it *Inter Linea* because I can cut right through the lines with it."

There was no answer.

Suddenly afraid that he'd really overstepped the bounds of good manners and rank, and that the dragon lay sulking far back in the cave, Artos peered through the gloom.

The cave was dark and silent and cold.

He walked a few steps farther, then stopped,

surrounded by the icy silence. Always before, even when the dragon was quiet, there was a sense of it, large and brooding, in the cave. But Artos knew, with a sudden certainty, that this time the cave was empty.

Still, he called out again in a more mannerly way, putting hope ahead of certainty. "Sir? Father dragon? Are you home?" He put up a hand to one of the hanging stones to steady himself and his sword clanged on the ground.

"It's me. Artos. Pendragon. Son of the dragon. Are you there?"

Then he laughed a forced little laugh that echoed peculiarly, like a demented dove's coo. "You've gone out on a little flight, right?"

It was the only answer that came to him, though the dragon had never once in their months together actually mentioned flying. But everyone *knew* that dragons had wings, great leathery wings stretched between mighty tendons. And wings, of course, meant flight.

Artos laughed again, but this time it was a hollow little chuckle, as if the dove were mourning. He turned toward the small light at the cave's entrance.

"I'll come back again tomorrow. At my regular time. And I'll show you the sword then. I will. I promise." He said it out loud, just in case the dragon's magic and wisdom extended to retrieving words left in the still cave air. "Tomorrow."

9

Friends

But Artos didn't go back to the cave the next day, for the pattern had been subtly altered and, like a weaving gone awry, couldn't be changed back to the way it had been without a weakness in the cloth.

First of all, there was the sword. It changed Artos' standing with the other boys and they invited him to practice with them. He understood that, with the sword, he was no longer a child to them, a child to be teased or ignored at will. With the sword he was immediately raised to the status of a young man, eligible to be a partner in their games, if not an altogether equal partner.

Sword practice was not, of course, with swords but with stiff willow wands and under the watchful eye of the Master of Swords, a burly, brutish man whose broad arms were seamed with old scars.

It turned out that Artos, being small, was compensatingly quick. He was able to turn and duck and roll away from blows that caught Cai on the shoulder and elbow and thigh, to the trumpeting encouragement of the Master. After Artos got the hang of it, he beat Cai soundly.

However, his elation was short-lived. Bedvere beat him by simply overpowering him and Lancot beat him with smooth, liquid strokes that Artos could only admire. Still, he was one of them now, and the dragon's familiar wisdoms seemed like nothing when compared to the unaccustomed and wonderful rioting of real friends.

He spent both his small morning break and his longer afternoon break with his new friends, his voice roughening in their company, his language desperately off-color and mean. Many of the swears he used he didn't even understand, but he borrowed them from the others and used them with fierce abandon.

At dinner he amazed the boys with stories about naked warriors in the heather and carpets flying high above great towered cities.

"You've made it up," Bedvere said with admiration, though previously he'd called any of Artos' stories lies.

Artos didn't deny it.

Then he stumped them with a dizzying succession of riddles, only one of which Lancot got, and that only because he'd heard it somewhere before recently.

"Do the cup game again," Cai urged, his face red with laughter from the riddles.

"Yes," Bed and Lancot chimed in. "The cup game."

Artos found three identical cups, no chips or chinks to mark them out, and though there was no pea, he borrowed Cai's crested ring. Six times he fooled them and not once did they check under *all* the cups, so sure that he'd never cheat. When Cai lost for the last time, he slapped Artos companionably on the shoulder and took back his ring.

"Well done, Art," he said, as if it had been

the others who were fooled by the game and
not he.

That was friendship indeed, Artos thought as
he went to bed that night, dreaming of his new
manhood counted in willow wands, swords, cup
games, naughty words, and lies.

As if she already knew about the change in
Artos' status, Lady Marion called all four of the
boys to her chambers in the morning. Since it
was a summons from the chatelaine herself, the
Masters of Hounds and Hawks couldn't fault Artos
for being late. He smoothed his fair hair down
carefully, paying special attention to the cowlick
in the front, and waited with Bedvere and Lancot
outside the door while Cai went in to see his
mother alone.

A minute later, Cai stuck his head out of the
door. "Hullo," he called. "All in."

They went in, Lancot in the lead, Bed next,
and last Artos conscious of the newness of his
position. He was determined to say nothing that
might be taken as a mistake.

Looking around as unobtrusively as he could,
Artos was awed by everything. There were floor-
to-ceiling hanging tapestries with picture-story

designs, many of which he recognized from the dragon's tales—Adam and Eve *with* fig leaves on one, the children of Pryderi on another, a third with what could only have been the alphabet of trees. He tried not to stare. There were cut flowers arranged in bowls and hanging pots of flowering plants, and a mix of rushes and dried verbena on the floor, all of which lent the room a sweet, fresh smell. *Women,* he thought with both admiration and envy, *have the best of it.* He wondered if his own mother had dwelled in such a room.

In a gown the color of new primroses, Lady Marion sat in a high carved chair whose back quite dwarfed her. An illuminated Bible rested on her lap. As the boys filed in, she closed the book and handed it to Cai, who set it on the lectern near the hearth. Waving the boys to stand before her, her rings winking at them in the sunlight, Lady Marion waited until they were fully at attention. Then she smiled.

"Good boys, and an especial welcome to you, young Artos. I understand from our Cai that you are become a man."

Artos bobbed his head and said, quite quietly in case it was the wrong thing to say, "I have a sword now, Ma'am."

"And so you do, with a fine watering down the blade," she said. "Cai says it looks like a rush of wind."

"Like dragon's fire, Ma'am," he said. Then, seeing her smile again, he wondered if he should have been silent. But her smile was sweet, not forced. *It's all right then*, he thought.

"You will need a new suit of clothes to go with your new state. More gentlemanly and less . . . less . . . kennel boy. Sylvia?" She turned and nodded to one of her maids, who stepped forward in a wave of perfume that made Artos quite dizzy. "Be sure and find something his size but allow for growth. He's small now, but young men grow so rapidly once they begin."

Artos felt his cheeks grow hotter with each word. It was bad enough being small and insignificant, but far worse having it pointed out in so public a fashion by a lady, especially in such gentle and caring tones. Fortunately, Lady Marion changed the subject. Not, Artos suspected, to spare his feelings but because the subject had been exhausted.

"Now there is to be a market fair in Shapwick next week and another three days after in Woolvington. Since it's but a short autumn till the

Holy Days are here, we must start thinking about gifts. Remembering, always, that not everyone here at *Beau Regarde* is Christian as Sir Ector and I and all of you are. We have some who still follow the Druids . . ."

"Old Linn," Cai whispered out of the side of his mouth.

Lady Marion ignored him, ". . . and some of the old soldiers, bless them, still drink bull's blood and worship Mithras, though I believe they do it less out of religious fervor than out of companionship. Old boys together. They think I don't know about their little meetings under the castle in that rabbit warren of rooms down there, but I do."

She seems to be saying it as a kind of warning, thought Artos. But Cai whispered to him, "Father has promised to take us all."

Artos glanced at him. *Us all.* Did Cai mean to include him, too?

"We shall therefore need silks and jewels and some good Scottish wool," Lady Marion concluded.

Lancot nudged Artos. "I thought all Scots went naked," he whispered.

"Only into battle, Lancot," said Lady Marion

83

smoothly. "They are perfectly well clothed at other times and their wool is the best in the known world."

"Yes, Ma'am," Lancot said, dimpling a smile at her.

"Now your father is out after that stag again, Cai." She rolled her eyes as if to admit silently that sometimes men could be a terrible burden. "And probably drinking himself into another attack of the gout, which he will blame on the weather or the wiliness of the white beast. So I daren't accompany you. *Someone* has to see to the running of this household. And poor old Merlinnus is bedridden with the miseries. He can't take you boys as he did last year. But you, Cai, are quite grown-up now. Can I expect you to guide these other three gentlemen as befits the son of Sir Ector and the heir to *Beau Regarde?*"

Bed nudged Lancot. "Good Old Linn, going sick like that."

Lancot bit his lips thoughtfully before nudging Artos.

But Cai, under his mother's direct scrutiny, stood straight and tall. "Yes, mother, you can count on me." He knelt and kissed her hand.

"And promise me you will be especially careful of young Artos. He's not been away from this castle since . . . since being brought here all those years ago. I would not have him lost or hurt for anything."

"*Not for anything, Mother,*" Cai assured her.

Artos didn't like the way he said it.

They managed to get out of Lady Marion's room with only one other nudge from Bed and several winks from Cai as he turned toward them, ushering them out with quick waves of his hands. They filed out as they had come in, with Cai in the lead and Artos at the tail.

When he looked over his shoulder for one last glance, Artos noticed a strange expression on Lady Marion's face. In that moment, he realized that she'd seen all the nudges and winks and yet was prepared to ignore them because there was a time in a young man's life when he had to make choices on his own. Yet that expression also said that she knew her son for a wastrel, Bed for a bully, and Lancot for a generous fool. She nodded gravely at Artos, as if they'd a secret between them, as if she were saying to him—only to him—

"They'll be boys all the rest of their lives, but I know I can trust *you*."

He didn't understand how he knew all that from a single glance, but he did. He nodded gravely back at her. Then one of the maids—the one with all the perfume, Sylvia—closed the door and Lady Marion was shut off from his sight.

10

At the Fairs

At the afternoon break they played at the wands again, and again Artos beat Cai. This time he beat Bedvere as well by dancing away from the powerful strokes and making Bed look like a clumsy bear. Before he could have a go at Lancot, all three ganged up on him and pushed him to the ground, and the Master of Swords never protested.

Cai stuck a wand right at his throat, so hard it hurt. Bed lashed his arms twice on each side until Lancot pushed him away. But all the time

Artos never cried "Hold," and there'd been not even a hint of tears in his eyes, only a bright, blazing anger.

They let him up then and brushed him off, admiring him for his courage. The Master of Swords, his scarred arms folded in front of his chest, grunted his approval as well.

"Good show," Cai said, throwing his arm around Artos' shoulder. "And no blubbing. My mother wouldn't be worried about you if she'd seen *that!*"

Bedvere's only comment was a beneficent growl.

It was Lancot who whispered, "Never mind them. They won't bother you again now that you've shown your true colors. Tell us another story."

So he told them about the men in the Indies walking about on their hands, as if the beating had never happened, as if both his arms weren't striped with stinging red welts and a bead of black blood didn't rest like a jewel in the hollow of his throat. He'd never mention them ganging up on him, would not even allude to it. That's how such games were played, and he knew it without having to be told. Besides, they genuinely seemed to like him now. So everything really *was* all right.

He forwent dinner to go back to the dragon's cave. He carried no bowl of gravy, for he was still angry with the dragon for going off like that without a word. But he did bring the sword, sheathed at his side.

"And if there's wisdom in *that*," he muttered to himself as he scrambled over the stone outcroppings, "it's that I, at least, keep promises." He conveniently ignored the fact that he was a day late in keeping this one. A marsh harrier screamed a kind of punctuation to his mutterings.

The cave entrance seemed even darker and more uninviting than usual. Inside, it was silent as a tomb. But Artos had worked himself up to such a pitch of anger at the miserable wyrm's desertion that he was glad the place was empty. He expended several minutes calling the dragon some of the awful names he'd learned at swordplay the day before—*canker*, *pismire*, *firebrat*, *chinch*—and felt better immediately. The cave echoed loudly with the swears.

When the sound of them was done, Artos smiled feebly. "If you can go off without telling me," he whispered into the black, unforgiving chamber, "I can go off without telling you."

Then he set his chin, turned his back to the

cave, and walked slowly along the path to *Beau Regarde*, the weight of the sword causing him to cant to one side.

The journey to the market towns was to take a fortnight, though they packed as if going for a full month. The preparations themselves seemed to take as long. They packed and repacked the saddlebags, counted and re-counted the monies Lady Marion set out for them, and listened seven times over to their instructions. Artos even suggested to the other boys that their heads were packed as tightly as their bags, and they adopted that as their motto for the journey.

"Instructions from Lady Marion, instructions from Cook, instructions from the Master of Swords . . . and still this," Cai said, his face narrowing into its pout. By *this* he meant the four soldiers sent along as bodyguards.

It isn't so much a boy's trip as one of those caravans in far Araby the dragon spoke of, Artos thought. But he gloried in it anyway.

As they rode along, their cheeks were polished apple red by the cold autumnal winds. On the second day the weather broke and gray clouds rode sullenly over the brooding Mendip Hills. The

leaves and grass seemed a darker green than before, and that was when the rain actually started,
lightly at first like a fine mist. Then, as if the
heavens had been slit open with a knife, rain tor-
rented down.

They sheltered as best they could in a copse
of trees, the horses stomping restlessly under
the drip-drip-dripping from the overhanging
branches. There was no lightning, and Artos alone
was relieved. The dragon had told him a man
could die struck by lightning and that lightning
sought the high point, like a tree. The dripping
of the rain down the back of his neck was all
part of the adventure. Even the discomfort
seemed fun, though Cai complained bitterly and
long, as if the rain had been sent just to plague
him.

At Shapwick there was a junior tournament
for boys under sixteen. The other three signed
up at once, but Artos held back. He'd really only
worked with wands and not his sword, though
he'd brought it with him, of course. And he was
curiously reluctant to use it against another person in fun. But he was loud in his cheering for
his three friends, so much so that many people

turned to smile at him for his boisterous loyalty.

Cai was eliminated in the first round, but by a giant of a boy, so he didn't feel too terribly downcast. And when that giant was beaten in the final round by Bed, in a long and sweaty battle, Cai was positively elated.

Lancot won with the lance.

Artos was agog at the banners and drums and horns and—quite frankly—at the enormous numbers of people. The closest he'd ever come to seeing that many people in one place had been the last time the High King had visited Sir Ector, and that had been several years earlier, with scarcely a tenth of the crowd. He stored up the faces and the sounds and the smells to take back with him.

He especially liked the pie sellers and was nearly sick from eating six pork pies in quick succession, the hot, tangy sauce running down his chin. Luckily the pieman ran out of pies before Artos ran out of coins, and he spent the last of that day's coins to listen to a traveling troupe of players who told "The Conception of Pryderi" better than anyone he'd ever heard.

Five days later at Woolvington's wool fair, when they were settled at a fine inn, Cai kissed Olwen, a serving girl, and even told her that he loved her. But then, privately, he said horribly funny things about her to Bed and Lancot and Artos. Artos felt awful about it, but he couldn't bring himself to say anything to Cai. As Cai continued all evening to make jokes about the girl—about her fat ostler father and her ugly mother who was the inn's cook—Artos fell to remembering the way he'd treated poor garlicky Mag. He felt his chin sink lower and lower onto his chest and he wondered what to do. Since he didn't want to lose his new friends, he didn't protest, but he began to think a lot about the dragon's wisdoms.

It wasn't until their last evening at Woolvington fair, with Olwen sitting all unhappy by Cai's side and Cai winking broadly at his friends as if to remind them about his jokes at her expense, that Artos finally knew what he had to do.

He had been asked to sing and had gotten through several songs when he remembered one the dragon had taught him called "Olwen the Fair." It was a sad song, really, for in the end Olwen dies. But it was lavish in its praise for the song's Olwen, for her fair cheeks and eyes the blue of cornflowers. He sang it directly to Cai's wench, ignoring the smirks and giggles of the other boys. He let her know with the song that he, at least, honored her.

At the song's end Cai's yellow-haired Olwen was so touched, she gave Artos a kiss and went out of the room with her head held high. Cai was a bit annoyed at losing her. And the guards who had accompanied them did not understand.

"You've got a sweet voice, young Art," said one. "Too bad it'll soon be changing."

Artos smiled. His voice might change—but the message would not. Inwardly he thanked the dragon, and he nodded at the guard.

They started home the next day, and something peculiar happened. Artos lapsed into a long, unbreakable silence. Though he'd been their main entertainment on the road there—telling stories and singing songs—it was as if he'd suddenly been bewitched.

"Tell us a tale," Cai begged. "You haven't told one all day, and your tales make the road shorter."

They all shouted their agreement. "Another tale, Artos. Or a song."

He said nothing.

"Afraid of old Garlic Breath, then?" Cai asked

slyly. "At least Olwen's breath was sweeter, you have to give her that."

Artos sighed. So Cai had learned nothing. But Olwen, he knew, had been comforted. There was that.

By the time they passed by the town of Meare and were on their way toward Shapwick, they were all teasing him about Mag. He was so sunk in misery by that time, he didn't ask how they knew. He just assumed, miserably, that all his exploits at the castle were well known. Except, of course, his time with the dragon.

"He's afraid of my new sword and what I'll do to him at our next game," Bed said, patting the sword he'd won in the tourney, the old one with the snakes put aside.

"Or my lance," Lancot said brightly, though clearly he didn't believe that to be the case at all.

But Artos kept his silence. He kept it despite their attempts to wheedle him into a story or song or riddle or the name of the one who'd bewitched him. In the attempt they listed every girl they knew as the cause. And then, for good measure, they added the names of the hard-handed men he might be worrying about back home: the Masters of Hawks and Hounds, the Master of Swords, Magnus Pieter, Sir Ector, even sickly Old Linn.

Of course they never mentioned dragons. They didn't know one lived near the castle, and Artos had certainly not breathed a word of its existence to them.

But it was the dragon that obsessed him and had ever since he'd used one of its wisdoms to help the girl Olwen. With each mile closer to the castle, he remembered the total and utter silence of the empty cave and how he'd neglected the dragon out of anger, out of self-righteous pique. He wondered if the dragon had returned; if it was angry that he hadn't come by with its daily meat. He wondered if it even cared, if it had *ever* cared, really, or if he'd only been a distraction.

Artos Pendragon. Son of the dragon. He knew he was no man's real son. He was a fosterling, fatherless as well as motherless. His hand went to the bag under his tunic. *Even more fatherless,* he told himself. *At least I've a ring from my mother. I've nothing belonging to the man who sired me. The only father I've had—if only for a few short months—has been a clanking, hot-*

breathed, storytelling dragon. And I left that dragon to play at willow wands with a trio of unruly, bulky, illiterate boys.

Each night of the return trip, Artos dreamed about the dragon's cave, with its entrance staring down from the tor like the empty eye socket of a long-dead beast. It hadn't been a happy dream, a dream about fathers. It had been a horrible, repeating nightmare, and he was afraid of what it meant.

They arrived home to find that Sir Ector had returned before them, sick with the gout as Lady Marion had foretold. He was sitting by the great hearthfire with his right foot wrapped in toweling and elevated on a stool. He was unhappy and distracted by pain, unable to greet them with any warmth.

The castle was busy with unpackings and there was such a bustling about that *Beau Regarde* felt, for a little while at least, like a truly great manor house. Of course that meant that no one paid much attention to the boys.

Having been outside, having seen the tournament at Shapwick and the wool fair at Woolvington, having passed large inns and other castles,

Artos understood for the first time what a really small place Sir Ector's castle was. And the peculiar thing about *that* knowledge was that he knew, at the same time, how much he treasured *Beau Regarde* for its very smallness, for its ordinariness, for its familiarity. It was the one thought that pierced through his misery. All the traveling, all the wild tales he'd told, all the sights he'd seen, made him happier to be here—at home.

The boys helped unpack their bags of presents and carted them up to Lady Marion's rooms. She, in turn, fed them wine and hot milk and cakes: little buttered breads, buns sticky with sugared icing, and cakes shot full of poppyseeds.

Her minstrel, a handsome boy except for his wandering left eye, sang a number of songs while they ate. They were all familiar to Artos—he'd learned them from the dragon. He hummed along quietly, but he ate nothing. His stomach suddenly hurt.

It was well past sundown before Lady Marion finished thanking them and let them go at last.

"Let's play at draughts," Cai said.

"Artos can tell us a story while we play," Bed suggested.

Lancot added, "Better yet, let's teach Artos to play."

But he brushed their suggestions aside and ran down the stairs. When they called after, he ignored them and only the startled ends of their voices followed him.

He hammered on the gate, closed since sundown, until the guards lifted the great latch and pushed the gates apart just enough to let him slip through. Then he raced across the moat bridge, where muddy lumps in the water were the only signs of life.

As he ran into the deepening dark, down the familiar path, he held his hand over his heart, cradling the two pieces of cake he'd slipped inside his tunic. He hadn't time to spare to beg stew from Mag, even though he wouldn't have begrudged her a kiss now. Not if it made her happy. He hoped the seed cakes would please the dragon. He didn't think for a moment that the dragon had actually starved to death without his poor offering of stew. That dragon had existed for many years before Artos had appeared by happy accident in its cave. No—it wasn't the size of the stew but the fact of it. Just as it wasn't the jewel

99

under the cup but the fact that the onlooker believed it had been put there.

He stubbed his toe on the second outcropping because of the dark, hard enough to force a small mewing sound from between his lips, though the blow hadn't hurt as much as Cai's wand at his throat. Only he hadn't been expecting his toe to be stubbed and he *had* expected Cai to do exactly as he'd done with the wand.

When he started up the tor, he found the path slippery and that made climbing difficult, especially with one hand over his tunic to keep the cakes from falling out.

He got to the mouth of the cave at last and was relieved to hear heavy, ragged breathing echoing off the wall; relieved, that is, until he realized it was only the sound of his own panting.

"Dragon!" he cried out, his voice a sudden broken misery. *What if the dragon really had counted on the stew? What if the dragon were starving? What if the dragon were dead?* "Dragon!"

11

Son of the Dragon

For a long, horrible moment the cave was silent, an awful, palpable, black silence. Then there was a small moan and an even smaller glow, like dying embers that have been breathed upon just one last time.

"Is that you, my son?" The voice was scarcely a whisper, so quiet the walls could not find enough substance to echo.

"Yes, dragon," Artos said, horribly relieved. "It's me."

"It is *I*," the dragon corrected feebly. "Did you . . . did you bring me any stew?"

"Only two seed cakes."

"I like seed cakes."

"Then I'll bring them over to you."

"Noooooooooooo." The sound held only the faintest memory of that old, powerful voice.

But Artos had already started toward the back of the cave, one hand cradling the cakes against his chest, the other well in front to guide himself around the treacherous overhanging rocks. He was halfway there when he stumbled against something and fell heavily to his knees. Feeling around, he touched a long, metallic, curved blade.

Fearing the worst, he cried out, "A sword! Oh, dragon, has someone else been here? Has someone killed you?" His mind pictured Bedvere bumbling about in the dark, blade in hand, though he knew that Bed had been along with him on the journey. Perhaps one of the guards, or even Sir Ector himself on the hunt, had stumbled across the cave, though he knew in his heart the guards never chanced the peat bogs and the hunt had taken place west of Nethy in the deep forest, not across the fen so close to *Beau Regarde*.

Before the dragon could answer, Artos' hand traveled farther along the blade to its strange metallic base. It didn't feel like a sword at all. It felt like . . .

His hands told him what his eyes could not; his mouth spoke what his heart did not want to hear.

"The dragon's foot."

He leaped over the metal construct and scrambled across a small rocky wall. Behind it, in the glow of a brazier, lay an old man on a straw bed. Near him were tables containing beakers full of colored liquids—amber, rose, green, and gold. From the gold a small, steady stream of clouds issued forth. On the near wall was a maze of strange toothed wheels locked one onto the other, with polished wooden handles at either end. On the far wall was a great door, carved with strange runes. By the old man's head was an open-mouthed cylinder with a long tubing attached, snaking all the way down to an opening in the wall.

The old man raised himself wearily onto one arm and tried to set his mouth into a welcoming smile.

"Pendragon," he said, though a tremor in his

yellowish lips betrayed him and slurred the syllables. "Son."

"Old Linn?" Artos was suddenly shaking with anger. The dragon, so powerful, so dangerous, so all-wise—his secret father, his teacher, his friend—was *this*? On *this* he'd expended his fear, his faith, his . . . his love? If anyone ever found out, he'd be a joke. And what kind of wisdom had he gotten if its fount was a feeble, dying spring? He felt sick.

"You are a cheat. A *pismire*. A *chinch*." The boyish swears rose easily to his lips.

The apothecary forced himself into a sitting position, his robes falling open to display knobby legs with prominent veins running from knee to ankle like old, meandering blue rivers. In a late attempt at dignity, he clutched the two sides of the robe together and began to speak quickly, before Artos' anger had time to set into rigid hate.

"Listen, boy. There was once a mighty king who would know Truth and so he put on a beggar's robe and traveled all over the world in his search."

His voice was quieter than the dragon's had ever been, of course, but the rhythms were the same. Artos cursed himself that he'd never noticed. Yet, without willing it, he was pulled into the old man's tale.

"The king looked along the seacoasts and in the quiet farm dales," Old Linn continued. "He went into the country of lakes and across the sandy deserts. He went into the uninhabited forests and through the noisy towns, seeking Truth. And at last, one dark night, in a small cave atop a high tor, he found her. *Truth*. Truth was a wizened old woman with but a single tooth left in her head. Her eyes were cloudy and her hair greasy, lank strands. But when she called him into her cave, her voice was low and lyrical and pure and that was how he knew he'd found Truth at last."

Artos nodded, caught himself, tried to recapture his hot anger, and stirred uneasily.

The old man went on. "He stayed with Truth a year and a day. A year and a day learning all she had to teach. And when his time was done, he said, 'My Lady, Truth, I must go back to my own kingdom now and serve my own people as I have served you. For a king is but his land's servant. Still, I would do something for you in exchange for all you have given me.'" Old Linn

105

hesitated and the silence grew between them until it was almost a wall.

"Well?" Artos said at last.

The old man was silent.

"Well—what did she answer? You can't stop a story there."

Old Linn was careful not to smile. Gently he said, "She told him: 'When you speak of me, tell your people that I am young and beautiful.'"

For a long moment Artos said nothing. Then he barked out a short, hollow laugh. "Another cheat. So much for the truth!"

Old Linn patted the mattress next to him, an invitation Artos ignored. "Tell me, Artos Pendragon, would you have listened these seven months to an old apothecary with a tendency to fits? A man you were convinced hated you? A man without discernible power or potency?"

Artos shrugged.

"Or would you listen only to a dragon, fiery, fierce, fair-minded, strong, full of arcane and extraordinary wisdoms who—quite possibly—liked you for yourself alone? Quite possibly loved you as a son? *Pendragon.*"

"You didn't tell me the truth," Artos said. "And that's the whole of it."

There was a moment of silence. Then the old man said, "I didn't lie. You *are* the dragon's son."

12

The Dragon's Boy

Artos took a good look at the sick old man and cried out in pain, in anger, in disbelief, and in despair. "Noooooooooo."

The words were still echoing off the cavern walls when he ran out and down the darkened path, heedless of the rocks in his way. He stumbled off into the marshy cushions of moorland, startling a swan that rose white and mute from a pool of standing water.

He found himself suddenly knee deep in that

same pool, surrounded by duckweed and water mint, his mind as muddy as the pond.

How could Old Linn be my father? My father should be a strong, fair-minded knight, not a . . . a . . . He remembered the words the old man had used: *An old apothecary with a tendency to fits.* Without thinking, he put his hand on the bag, feeling the ring roll around beneath his fingers. *And won't they all laugh at me—Cai, Lancot, Bed. Fathered by an old man. A secretive old man. A crazy old man. A lying old man.*

His feet had begun to go numb in the cold water, and he edged toward the clumps of water violets rimming the pool. Tangling his hands in the vegetation, he hauled himself up and out, onto some sort of strange wooden pathway.

He knew what it was, one of the Old Paths. He'd heard of the lake folk who'd *walked the ancient planks* but had never actually seen any remains before.

Taking his boots off and dumping out the water in them, he sat for a long time thinking about the ancient folk, the ones who'd built the walkways all across the fens. They'd known so much—and now their knowledge was gone. Only bits and pieces—like the walkways—remained.

And their stories, he suddenly reminded himself because he was, at the core, an honest boy. *Stories the dragon had told him. The dragon. Old Linn.* He made a face.

At last he pulled the wet boots back on, stood, and looked around. It was fully night. The moon was directly overhead. How long had he been sitting out on the moors? One shouldn't stay here all night. There were the peat hags to worry about, of course. And the faeries, though they dwelled mostly on the High Tor. And the cold. But there was no dragon, he knew that now. There was only a feeble old man.

He stared up at the moon. It was trembly and yellow faced and he could make out eyes, a nose, a slash of mouth. It reminded him of Old Linn. *Merlinnus*, Lady Marion had called him. He hated the old man for what he'd done. For lying about the dragon. Yet he *hadn't* lied about the wisdoms. Not really. Artos sighed.

For it had been the wisdom that had gotten him his sword. And the wisdom that had won him his new friends. And the wisdom that had helped him understand Olwen's condition. And Mag's.

Why, he thought suddenly, *without that wisdom I'd be no better than a bulky, unruly, illiterate boy.* He smiled ruefully, remembering when that had, in fact, been all he'd wanted to be.

He stretched and then, carefully, walked back along the remnants of the wooden pathway and found the place where he'd stumbled away from his old path. It was well marked by moonlight. His feet had a bit of feeling in them again, which made him acutely aware of just how uncomfortable wet boots could be. The cake had mashed itself against the inside of his shirt. He wondered what it would taste like now. Setting his mouth in a line, he turned toward the cave.

He knew he could just go back to the castle, dusting out the cake crumbs for the moat tortoise or Boadie and her pups. He could settle down in his featherbed and forget the old man lying yellow-mouthed in the cave. But if the dragon had taught him one wisdom, it had to be this: *Bring gravy every day and confront your worst fear.* Well, he didn't have any gravy, but he still had a whole lot of unspoken fears: of being laughed at, of being

111

made a fool, of having a man like Old Linn as a father.

The path up to the cave was familiar even in the dark. When he reached the entrance, he took a long, shuddering breath, and called into the blackness.

"I—am—*not*—your—son." Not asking—telling. There. It was said. So why did he feel so awful having said it?

There was an answering sigh. "True," came the old man's voice, drawing him back inside the cave.

Artos walked carefully, avoiding both the metal foot and the hanging stones. He came around the wall and saw that Old Linn was still lying on the straw bed. The great carved door on the far wall was now ajar, as if he'd tried to leave and couldn't quite manage it.

"True? Then why did you call me your son? Why did you give me that awful lie?"

"True, not true. The storyteller does not ever tell the truth baldly. I tell you that you are the son of a dragon. Pendragon. That is truth made young and beautiful. You knew you didn't spring from the loins of a real dragon. Boadie bears pups. Lady Marion bears boys. Dragons bear dragons.

That is truth baldly. But wisdom . . ." He smiled weakly.

Artos was not amused. "You said I was *your* son and you are a man."

"I am a Druid priest, chaste, sworn never to marry nor to sire a child, all so that I may perform my magicks and study my particular wisdoms."

"A priest?" The surprise in Artos' voice was undisguised. The only priest he'd ever known was Father Bertram.

"I did not sire you, but I bore you," the old man said. "Answer that riddle, if you can."

Artos answered warily, "Boadie bears pups. Lady Marion bears boys. Dragons bear dragons. And . . ."

"I bore you. . . ."

Artos suddenly smiled. "You bore me away from some place. That's it, isn't it?"

The old man was silent for a long moment, as silent as the dragon had been for every correct answer.

"From whom did you bear me away?" Artos asked at last.

"From your mother, before your birth father ever saw you," Old Linn said. "And carried you

113

to Sir Ector's castle. And kept watch over you ever since. Is that not a fine fathering?"

Artos felt the anger rise up in him again, like spring sap. "A silent father," he said quietly. Then louder, "A deceitful father."

"I was sworn to secrecy, my boy," Old Linn said, struggling to sit up. "Sworn to keep your name and lineage until you proved yourself worthy of it."

"And if I did not?" The question paused in the air between them.

"Ah, well." The old man coughed. "The dragon and I were meant to see that you became worthy."

"But I found the dragon by accident," Artos said.

"Did you?" the old man asked.

"Didn't I?" But then he remembered Boadie's flight and the tracks leading toward the cave and wondered. "I was to get wisdom," he whispered.

The old man smiled. "Just so. Wisdom. Already you had some knowledge. Your childish promise showed when you learned your letters with ease."

The bag seemed to grow warm against Artos' chest. He reached up to stroke it.

"Such ease of learning was part of your inheritance."

My inheritance, Artos thought. *And Old Linn the only one who can tell me of it.*

"But," the old man continued, "suddenly you reached your springtide and you stopped growing into that promise. You grew instead into a longing for the wisdom of sword and lance. That, of course, I didn't have to give." His voice seemed to sigh into the air. "What was I to do? I enlisted that fool of a smith and that wraith of a hound, and by Lady Marion's good graces as well, you *accidentally* came upon a dragon. Or perhaps you did not. There is wisdom to be found in happy accidents, you know. It is the wisdom of the Land of Serendip."

Artos' hand dropped from the bag. He closed his eyes to keep tears from starting. "But I *believed* in that dragon."

Old Linn chuckled. "It was a good dragon, wasn't it? I made it myself."

"I *loved* that dragon."

"And yet you left it without a good-bye."

Remembering the silence of the cave and how readily he had turned to his noisy new friends, Artos was nevertheless stung by the unfairness

115

of the accusation. "I did come back," he whispered. "The second day." He walked over to the straw bed and knelt by its side. "I did try."

The apothecary put his hand on Artos' head, then croaked out, "Did you . . . did you bring any of that stew?"

"I . . ." The tears, so long checked, were falling now. "I brought you seed cakes."

"I like seed cakes," Old Linn said.

"They're awfully mashed."

"Even so," the old man said. "But couldn't you have gotten any stew from Garlic Mag?"

Artos felt his mouth drop open. "How did you know about her?"

The old man smiled, showing terrible teeth, and whispered, "I am the Great Riddler. I am the Master of Wisdoms. I am the Word and I am the Light. I Was and Am and Will Be." He hesitated, reached up, and pulled the cylinder toward him, speaking directly into its open mouth. "I AM THE DRAGON!"

The words ran down into the tubing and issued forth out of an opening in the wall so loudly that the cave was awash with echoes.

Artos picked up the old man's hand and held it. He was amazed at how frail the hand was.

His bones, Artos thought, *must be as hollow as the wing bones of a bird. As hollow as the wing bones of a dragon. A bird. A dragon. Merlinnus.* He thought about the hawks in the castle mews, one of them a little merlin. Smiling, he mouthed the words "Perhaps you are the dragon" to Old Linn's fingers, but the old man didn't hear it.

"Look," the apothecary said, pointing to the door in the far wall, barely illuminated by the brazier's fading light. "Through that door, Pendragon, are the men you must learn to lead. With passion. With fairness. With wisdom. Are you bold enough to do it?"

Artos looked not at the door but at the carved signs of power on it. In the flickering light, the runes seemed to move and change even as he watched.

Suddenly he didn't feel very bold. He didn't have the wisdom to even read any of the warnings set out in the wood. All he had were a few stories, a great longing, some riddles and songs, and a game of cups and peas. How could *those* be enough?

He turned and looked at Old Linn. The old man's eyes caught the light of the brazier and they burned like the eyes of a dragon.

Artos squared his shoulders and whispered, "I cannot go alone, sir." He bent down, put his hands under Old Linn's arms, and pulled him gently to his feet. Then with his hand firm under the old man's elbow, he guided them both through the door.

As they passed beneath the lintel, Artos looked up. He could just make out a few of the words carved there. Something to do with kings, once and in the future. He shook his head and smiled a small smile.

Past the door was a warren of hallways and rooms. From somewhere ahead, Artos heard the chanting of many men. *Celebrating with Mithras,* he thought, *just as Lady Marion said.* He wrinkled his nose briefly at the thought of drinking bull's blood and wondered if Sir Ector was among the men, his bandaged foot upon a chair. Mithras, the Druids, Christianity, the fenfolk—wisdom, it seemed, came in many forms and from the mouths of many gods. It was seen placed under many different cups. How one *used* the wisdom was what really counted. He smiled.

"I think I am beginning to understand, sir," Artos said.

"Understand?"

"About wisdom."

"Are you now?"

"Yes. You may not *look* like a dragon, all teeth and nails. But you *are* a dragon indeed."

"A very *old* dragon," the apothecary warned.

"How. . ." Artos' voice was suddenly troubled. "Just *how* old, sir?"

"Five of your lifetimes, my boy. But then, my own father reached one hundred."

"One hundred lifetimes?"

Old Linn smiled. "One hundred years."

"Good." Artos breathed deeply, then added quickly in his head. "That means you have at least two of my lifetimes to go. I would not have you die just yet. I have not finished getting my wisdom."

He thought the old man chuckled, but perhaps it was a simple clearing of the throat.

"Can I have that piece of cake now?" Old Linn asked.

"It's two pieces, really. And quite mashed."

"Two pieces then, one for each lifetime to come."

"They really should be shared," Artos said.

Old Linn looked directly at him and drew himself up to his full height. "But I . . ." he said, his voice suddenly hard, "*I* am the Dragon."

119

"And I . . ." Artos replied, reaching into his shirt and scraping together one piece of the cake, which he pushed toward Old Linn's mouth before taking the second piece for himself, "*I* am the Dragon's Boy."

TALBOT HILL SCHOOL